SIDESHOW

ALLEY

Edited by Jo Seysener

A Drabbles Anthology

First edition

Cover art by Danielle Doolittle [DoElle Designs]
www.doelledesigns.wix.com

Edited by Jo Seysener

ISBN 978-0-6486947-0-0

CONTENTS

Copyright © 2019 by Little Quail Press III

Foreword XI

Neen Cohen 1

    You're Home Now 2

    Her Smell For Magic 3

    Scared Enough 4

    Why So Exhausted 6

    The Apprentice 7

Cassandra Kelly 9

    Attention 10

    Duck 11

    Freak Show 12

    Isolation 13

    Peep Show 14

Joanne Creed 15

    Beppo 16

    Funhouse 18

    Magisto's Puppets 20

    Malloran and Phyllida 21

    Merry-Go-Back 22

A Michael Blair 25

    Petey 26

    Aztec Man 28

    The Platter Clean 30

Freaks Like Us 32

On a Roll 33

Craig Thomson 35

Ground Zero 36

Moths Ta a Flame 37

At Hand 38

Vector 39

The Gift Given 40

Jo Seysener 41

Eye Above All 42

High Riders 43

Next, Please 44

Coffee and Floss 45

Fire In The Sky 47

Jacinta Goodsell 49

The Summoning 50

Do You Feel Lucky 51

Pick Pocket 52

Survivor's Account 53

A Taste Of Toffee 54

Jem McCusker 55

Chained 56

Delight 57

Two Hands 58

A Penny For Your Thoughts 59

Death Hymn 60

K B Elijah 61

    Sliver 62

    The Clever Ones 63

    Spectres 64

    Ducks and Snacks 65

    Shinning, Shimmering, Splendid 66

Zoe Marks 67

    Dante 68

    Cloud 69

    The Big Top 70

    Mum's Carnival 71

    The Royal Carnival 72

Shan L. Scott 73

    Ferris Wheel 74

    Clowns 75

    Merry-Go-Round 76

    Jack In The Box 77

    Mirrors 78

Monica Schultz 79

    Freak Show 80

    Hunted 81

    Sea Monkeys 82

    The Black Pen 83

    When the Lights Go Out 84

Jayne Vidler 85

    The Carnival Night Guard 86

Fated Tarot...87

Show Bag Treats...88

The Hustle...89

The Carnival of Souls.......................................90

J A Henderson..91

All Dogs go to Heaven.......................................92

Harry Fritsch...93

Big Boy Rides...94

Inside Out Lunch..95

Inflamed Prices...96

The Violinist...97

Above and Beyond..98

Jasmine Jarvis..99

Authentic Oddities...100

Opening Night Nerves.......................................101

See The Fire...102

Sideshow Alley...103

The Tattooed Man...104

Sofia Aves...105

Facades and Flowers..106

Practice Rounds..107

Aim True...108

Nicole Harvey..109

Joey's First Ride..110

Haunted House..111

A Child's Eyes...112

Silvie de Wilde 113

    Funny Face 114

    Magnus Moreau's Fine Statue Show 115

    Dancing Bear 116

    The Fortune-Teller 117

    The Judas Kiss 118

Contributors 119

    Danielle Doolittle 119

    Rozie Marshall 120

Acknowledgements 121

X

FOREWORD

Books are everywhere in our lives. We read them for leisure, we study them at school. Some people want to write them. Many never know where to start, or how.

This anthology showcases authors from Ipswich, Queensland, Australia. Some are unpublished, just finding their feet. Other are emerging writers, some with many books to their name.

Every author starts somewhere.

Our authors have captured the heart of Sideshow Alley. Enter a world of bright lights, constant chatter. Overpowering popcorn and fairy floss aromas, the call of Carnies selling their wares.

Journey into a world of dazzling mirrors, deep into the Haunted House. But don't get lost...when the gate closes, Sideshow Alley darkens. In the shadows wait...

Well, I wouldn't hang around to see. Would you?

Cheers,

Jo Seyener

Neen Cohen

Neen Cohen is an emerging LGBTQI and speculative fiction author. She has a Bachelor of Creative Industries and is a member of the Springfield Writers Group.

Neen lives in Brisbane with her partner, son and fur babies. She loves to roam cemeteries, botanic gardens, and construction sites and can often be found writing while sitting against a tree or tombstone.

https://wordbubblessite.wordpress.com

YOU'RE HOME NOW

Taking a deep drag of nicotine, the fortune teller watched teens giggle by, ignoring her faded sign. Bright lights and obnoxious sounds pulled their attention elsewhere.

All but one.

'Are you free to read?'

The girl stood, a shimmering image of a different world.

'What are you?'

The girl's bottom lip quivered.

'That's what I want to know.'

She lifted her long hair, just enough to show the old woman the pointed ears she hid.

'It's ok, child.'

The old woman's glamour dropped and the girl gasped to see horns curving around the fortune teller's head.

'You are home now.'

Her Smell For Magic

'Alice, come on now!'

'But mumma,' Alice pulled her mother back and pointed 'she's beautiful magic.'

'Oh, it's just an illusion.' Her mother pulled again on Alice's hand, but Alice kept looking at the woman floating the small balls instead of juggling them. The woman caught Alice's eyes, smiled and winked.

Alice smiled back before giving in to her mother's grip, skipping alongside.

Everything around her smelled of sugar and fruit, it would be her smell for magic. Her smile stayed.

Alice would spend the rest of her life searching for the woman who taught her how magic was real.

SCARED ENOUGH

'Oh please, baby.'

He closed his eyes and she squealed in delight. He had submitted.

'Two tickets please.'

The attendant handed over the tickets, eyes frozen on her boyfriend. She laughed. Everyone fell in love with him.

'Thanks, baby.'

'Alright.' He draped his arm across her shoulders.

She kissed his cheek as they stepped in to the haunted house.

'Scared enough baby?'

'They seem more scared than me.' She pouted.

'How about now?'

She looked up in to the face of a monster. Her scream was lost amongst the squeals of girls who would be safe in their beds tonight.

Why So Exhausted

During the show, she twisted her body with ease, hypnotising him. Cloak hiding the leotard, she now led him to her tent.

'What are you doing?'

Her eyes opened, pale and heavy. She knew he saw the air rippling around her lotus positioned body.

'They use my energy to reset the shows.'

'You are magic!'

She shrugged, an unhappy smile on her lips.

The tent flap fell closed as he stepped inside and sat to mirror her.

He entwined his fingers with her own and their eyes met.

'I have plenty of energy.'

The rippling air engulfed him as well.

THE APPRENTICE

Palming the man's wallet, Isiah felt no guilt. He had seen the man's adulterous sins dripping from him.

Justifying his thieving was easy, he could tell a person's sin by simply looking at them.

He walked away, humming. He blended easily with noise and lights, feigning excitement and awe for cheap tricks and games that didn't hold up in the light of day.

'Thanks.'

He paid for the toffee apple with stolen fare. He took a sticky bite and scoffed at the young boy clumsily applying their trade. But the kid was fast. Maybe it was time for an apprentice.

CASSANDRA KELLY

Cassandra Kelly is a steampunk author with a love of warm weather, blue skies, gardening, critical theory and zombie movies. She has an interest in history, particularly Australian colonial history and personal histories. Her first novel, 'The Green Wave', was released in 2019.

https://cassandrakellyauthor.com/

https://www.facebook.com/CassandraKellyAuthor/

ATTENTION

The colours capture my attention, the moving clown heads with their open mouths, and the calling of the spruiker have me transfixed. I look for my little sister.

She turns to look at me, red hair, freckles, ice-cream cone in hand, melting, running down her wrist, a spot of white on her nose, holding the hand of... That's not Mummy. Where is she going? I want to go with her, instead I run to find Mummy, tugging at her hand, she's talking to a friend, she won't listen.

Olive is gone. Mummy listens now, but we never see Olive again.

DUCK

The ball flies high and hits a prize on the third shelf. The man urges me on. My boyfriend, grinning, tells me to aim at the ducks, not the fluffy toys.

I squint as I aim, waiting for the moment. The ducks move by. I pick one, arm drawn back, and I throw again. The ducks are safe as the ball sails once more over their tin heads.

"You quack me up," laughs my boyfriend.

A shout behind me, "Stop, thief! He's got my bag!"

I aim at the thief but my boyfriend is in the way. He doesn't duck.

FREAK SHOW

The limbless man climbs onto his stool, hands grasping from his shoulders. His bare feet protrude from the bottom of his torso, toes gripping the legs of the stool, and he squirms into place.

The crowd enters the tent. He picks out individuals as they stare at him—the man in the expensive suit who loves money more than his family; the timid woman with the fading bruise around her eye standing frightened beside her husband; the aging woman with the plastic face clutching at her youth.

Each day a different crowd of people, yet still the same freak show.

ISOLATION

I was lonely and Sideshow Alley was quiet. Dejected after the end of a relationship I stood in the doorway of the fortune teller's tent. "Come in," said the old woman. I paid her and spoke of my misfortune. She stared into her crystal ball. "I can see a period of isolation, without men. You need it."

I stared into the ball and cried. She hugged me. I said, "This is how my last relationship ended," and I stabbed her. She didn't see that coming — nor I the police.

The padded cell is isolating and there are no men here.

PEEP SHOW

An intriguing back alley beckoned me. 'Madame X-ray's magic spectacles', read the sign; 'Your very own peep show. One hour - two shillings. Half price for women.' I couldn't resist and paid my shilling to the pretty door girl. She handed me a set of strange goggles and directed me to a glass booth in the centre of the room.

"To prevent touching." She winked.

I put on the goggles. Mirrors lining the walls reflected my nakedness but I could feel my clothes remained on. Men filed into the room, looking at me, smiling, smirking. The goggles wouldn't come off.

JOANNE CREED

Joanne Creed is a children's and young adult's author from Ipswich Queensland. She is author of the picture book, The Shop on the Corner. Joanne has had short stories published in the anthologies, 'It's Beginning to Look a Lot Like Christmas' and 'Spooktacular Stories – thrilling tales for brave kids'.

www.joannecreedauthor.com

www.facebook.com/joannecreedauthor

BEPPO

"Good luck!" he sneered.

Brawny arms hung Beppo up amongst dusty show toys: a garish pink plush teddy with the soul of a boy.

And a beating heart.

"Today might be your day."

Beppo regretted scamming the scammers. No prize haul was worth this.

Being dragged before the magician, trapped forever...

Unless he was won...

Chosen.

His keeper whistled, called, tossed a ball between grimy palms.

They came: jingling coins, round-eyed, hopeful. Toss after toss, and disappointment.

Until...

A Fluke! A grin.

"*YES!*"

Then, unbelievably, "That one!"

Inside the bear Beppo gasped. Lights spun, his stomach lurched.

And finally...

Freedom.

FUNHOUSE

"NO FUNHOUSE!" I say.

That means nothing to Nic. Only his dragging hands, and my laughing curses.

It means sneakers pounding up metal stairs, shaking floors, spinning rainbow tunnels, dips, clangs, ice cream truck music, flying plastic balls, and breathless whoops.

Then, oh God, the mirror.

And suddenly, no Nic and no funhouse.

Only me and Doppelganger.

Again.

Doppelganger's lips twist in a mocking grin, hands reaching out...

Outside I feel strange. Less me, and more him.

I don't know Nic, until he grabs my arm, spins me around.

My lips begin to twitch.

Ah help me... they won't stop.

MAGISTO'S PUPPETS

It was a quaint puppet theatre: wooden booth, scarlet velvet curtains, painted scenery. We were in for a treat, we thought.

The puppet master came: obscuring hat and scarf, swirling black cape.

And we weren't so sure.

Polly in the front row crept closer.

"They seem so real! The puppets!"

"And what of the tiny gold keys in their backs?" I asked.

A heavy hand fell on me, a voice growled at my ear.

"Nosy kids! You'll see!"

Next, two blurry days, plinking music, cheering faces.

Before I woke with a sore back, and marks on my hands and feet.

Malloran and Phyllida

Malloran rubbed aching shins.

"I'm sorry Mal. But we *owe* him."

"I know." He ground out; leaning back, as ten-foot legs miraculously grew to fill striped pants. "I'd do this forever before I'd let him have you."

Phyllida hunched, winced, as fantastic wings sprouted from her back. She turned, tears tracking down painted face. "I wish I'd never agreed..."

"We were starving, and it was my idea. Anyway, how could you know?"

"If these would hold, I'd fly away. Then you'd be free too."

"No. I'd miss your face." He gripped his pendant, her hand. "Besides, I have an idea..."

Merry-Go-Back

"Roller Coaster!"

"Mewwy-doh-wownd! *Pease?*"

Lola looks from pouting face to mother face.

"He'll run out of steam, later."

"Oh, okay."

They run, scramble up: fleet footed girl and cherubic infant.

"Horsey!"

"No, carriage like a prince!"

Lights flash on, music begins. Zander bounces, downy hair brushing her chin, chubby hands grabbing, smelling of fairy-floss and sauce.

"WEEEEEE!"

Then a queer jerk, and backwards...

Zander quivers, shrinks, disappears. Her own hands like Zander's: small, clutching.

"Mama?"

No mama. Only a girl in mama's sagging dress...

Now forwards again...

And stop.

Zander's back, crying. *"NO MEWWY-DOH-WOWND!"*

They jump into Mama's reaching arms.

A Michael Blair

My hometowns are Stanthorpe, West End and Ipswich. My CV is diverse—from factories to cattle stations, warehouses to laboratories, then 30 years in the public service. Outside 9-5, I cared for young people with autism and a man with advanced dementia. I write historical fiction, drabbles and poetry.

https://cockatoogate.com/

PETEY

A lion moaned as a unicyclist passed.

"Petey, there's a sucker born every minute."

"Yes sir, Mr Barnham," the little man agreed.

"Do you know why I like you?" asked Phineas, looking down.

"Cos I'm half a man and you only pay me half a wage?"

"Ha! I said that, didn't I? It was brandy talk. I pay you well enough."

"But it is funny."

"I like you because your name is my initials—PT."

"Funny too... Petey—PT." Petey chuckled.

Barnum strolled away, trailing a cloud of cigar smoke.

Petey's smile faded. "Brandy and cigars..." he muttered. "Chiselling jerk!"

Aztec Man

A man in a boater hat waved his cane.

"ROLL UP! THE LAST SURVIVING AZTEC! Direct from steamy African jungles."

"Look at him, what a dopey pinhead." The boy pointed and grinned.

"Keep it down, he can hear you," the girl urged.

"Who cares? He's too stupid to know."

"He's an exceptional specimen," remarked the Professor.

"Is he really an Aztec?" asked his companion.

"Of course not. It's a congenital aberration. Not common, but well known. I'd like to take some measurements."

They thinks I doesn't know, but I does, he thought, and a solitary tear rolled over his cheek.

THE PLATTER CLEAN

"You're losing weight, Fatima," he said with a frown.

"And you're putting it on, Jack," she replied.

They stared at their plates.

Jack picked up the pork chop with his fork. "Here, you take this, and I'll have your salad."

"Mm... The rind is divine." Fatima chewed with closed eyes.

"Pass the vinegar, love," Jack requested.

They finished their meals and left the tent in costume. Fatima wore an absurd pink tutu, and Jack was in tight singlet and child's lederhosen.

"LADIES AND GENTLEMAN," shouted the barker through his loudhailer, "I

GIVE YOU THE REAL JACK SPRATT AND HIS WIFE!"

Freaks Like Us

"The spiflocator imploded!" Jarnak declared.

"WE'RE CRASHING!" screamed Lobula.

"That field... those fabric structures. Put down there."

The craft slammed into the ground, violently pitching the pilots forward. It slid, bounced off a tree and stopped.

Jarnak shook his head and looked at his crewman. A lever pierced one eye, the others stared. "Farewell comrade. Many worlds we've trodden." Jarnak disembarked, his three arms limp with defeat.

"Holy crap! That was some landing, mate!" exclaimed a seven-foot man with horns. "I'm Shizmag from Proxima 83. Fear not, stranding on Earth isn't bad. We make a good living as sideshow freaks."

On a Roll

Carnival music trilled.

"I've never seen so much!" he exclaimed, rolling his enormous ball backwards with his feet.

"What kind of thing was that anyway?" she asked, pushing her own globe.

"It ain't from round here."

A clown almost stepped on them.

"WHOA! Even if we only get half, it'll last all season!"

"The rest will raise a hundred kids."

An elephant trumpeted.

"Quick! It's angry about us swiping it's shit!"

They rolled frantically. On a downhill slope, his ball ran over him several times.

"Are you ok?" she asked, horns twitching.

"Cripes! Thank the Lord High Beetle for exoskeletons!"

CRAIG THOMSON

Craig is a recovering procrastinator, devoted coffee addict and a relatively active member of the Ipswich Writers & Illustrators Group since late 2018. An avid reader, this is his first foray into publishing and first time dabbling in drabbles.

https://craigthomson85.wordpress.com/

GROUND ZERO

The lights, the noise, the smells. The show was back in town.

He'd waited a whole year, twelve long months, for it to return. For his chance to get to the bottom of it. To find out what they'd done to her.

He moved through the crowd, brushing past young teens and families, listening to their raucous laughter. Surrounded by their joy, he was alone.

Sideshow alley stretched before him, all glitz and glitter and glamour. Flashing lights, sirens calls. But below the brightly flashing surface was a dark canker. Something rotten. It was now or never.

He stepped forward.

Moths Ta a Flame

The lights, the noise, the smells. The show was back in town.

It was the same every time. Every stop they made, every town they went to - noise, dirt and dust. Teeming throngs packing the thoroughfares; coughing, spluttering, laughing and crying. Fools, the lot of 'em.

Still, they had their uses. What better way to spread the gifts of the Master? New plagues, new diseases, new infections. The ultimate live test.

He scanned the crowd, spotting a likely mark.

"What about you, miss? Are you brave enough to enter the Haunted House?" he called, stepping forward, guiding them in.

At Hand

The lights, the noise, the smells. The show engulfed him.

He let the crowd carry him, drawing him through sideshow alley, watching everything.

Then he saw it. The Haunted House was before him, just as he remembered it. The garish, strobing lights, the dense smoke, the electronic screams crackling through the outdated speakers. He stood back, sheltering beside an empty ticket booth and waited. Watched.

He watched the attendant single out a young couple in the crowd. He watched the attendant place a mark on her as she passed. This was it, what he had waited for. He stepped forward.

Vector

The lights, the noise, the smell. The show engulfed him.

He ushered a young couple through the large doors of the Haunted House, tracing a mark on the back of the girl as they entered the acrid cloud of chemical smoke. Once inside, the Others would see to her. They'd test the latest strain. It was clever, really. The Masters gifts were delivered, and no-one suspected a thing. Quite the opposite, everyone expected to get sick at the show.

He felt eyes on him. A dishevelled young man strode toward him, eyes burning, face set, fists clenched. He stepped back.

THE GIFT GIVEN

The lights, the noise, the smell. The show engulfed them.

"Bastards! What did you do to her?" He yelled, tackling the attendant through the doors and into the thick smoke.

A black boot crashed into his jaw. Bone shattered. He was pulled up, restrained, surrounded by faceless masks.

"This," the attendant spat, emptying a pressurised cannister into his face.

He breathed in the thick, acrid smoke.

His eyes burned. He coughed wetly, blackened blood splattering the floor.

The hands let go. He fell to the ground.

The couple stepped out into the lights, the noise, the smell. The girl coughed.

JO SEYSENER

Jo Seysener is a mum of three crazy small children and a cuddly, 32kg teacup puppy and her husband, who gives excellent feedback on story ideas at 2am. She writes picture books for children for Library for All and speculative fiction for adults. She is dabbling in romance this summer.

www.joseysener.com

www.facebook.com/joseysener

EYE ABOVE ALL

It's small, this world of lights and noise. Fenced in as the world goes on around it, unknowing the dramas within. Tears melting joy of ice cream smushed on the ground, adrenaline powered screams mingling with the overpowering music of rides and games.

Shunting to a halt, a long pause amidst the crowds. Boxes jump and swing, turning, pausing, but never ceasing. Taking them high, watching over it all.

Awe and love contained within my tiny carriages, so much in such a tiny space.

Until the lights turn off, leaving Sideshow Alley in darkness. I sleep, until they return again.

HIGH RIDERS

Tiny seats swirl, little feet hiking up and down to the rhythm of the music. Above the carnival children swing higher, music and lights blurring far below. A shoe flies, bouncing as it lands in the dust.

Seats flicker in the brightness with every turn, some filled, some empty. Swings stream in a great circle, rotating faster.

The beat thumps – not drums; the heartbeat of the ride.

Music slows, wires holding empty seats swaying gently as the ride descends. Excited cries, hands reaching through the fence. The gates open for new riders.

One smudged shoe sits lonely in the dirt.

NEXT, PLEASE

The greasy aroma of popcorn permeates the small van, warring with undertones of burnt coffee beans and the gut turning sweetness of fairy floss. Oil coats every surface, decorated with the dust and dirt of unpaved showgrounds. Her great belly bumps the counter as her gullet rises, the tiny life bumping back. She shoves the overcooked kernels into the cone, taking the customer's coins and sweaty notes.

She smiles, a slim, inane effort, leaning down in the pretence of grabbing more bags and retches quietly into a carton of cones. She misses them, just, and presents another smile.

Next, please.

COFFEE AND FLOSS

"What do you want to do first?"

"Dodgems!"

"Showbags!"

"No, clowns!"

"No, Dodgems!"

"Coffee."

"Righto, Mum's spoken, coffee first. Who wants some fairy floss?"

"Is it made from real fairies?"

"No, of course not. Fairies died out a long time ago." He smiles at the woman serving, "Coffee, and three bags of fairy floss, please. Here you go. And for you, Mum."

Mum smiles, taking the caffeine hit gratefully. He offers his eldest daughter a conspirator's smile and stage whispers, "They should call it elf floss now."

The serving woman tugs too-pale hair over pointed ears as she waves goodbye.

Fire In The Sky

"Look, Dad, that one's purple!"

"OOooh, that one looks like cockroaches crawling across the sky!"

"EEEWWW! MUM! He's touching me!"

"Wow, that was a big one."

Mum touches his damp arm, covered with a cold sweat.

"I don't like the smoke. Big BANG!" Smallest wails, tucking her head into Mum's shoulder.

"Fireworks can be scary. Why doesn't Dad take you for a walk over to the games?"

"Doesn't Daddy like fireworks?" Eldest frowns after her father and tiny sister toddling back to the bright lights. Mum smiles sadly and strokes her hair.

"Not all fireworks are lights and pretty colours."

JACINTA GOODSELL

Jacinta Goodsell is an emerging author who has just released her first poetry collection, Collective Cins. Just Say Yes is the first book in her new series and will be available soon along, with a Four Quills anthology. She writes dark romance, mystery, and thrillers with a dash of humour.

Instagram: @cinnabunreads
Facebook: @jgoodsellauthorpage

THE SUMMONING

The witches gathered around the unlit pyre, eager to see in another decade.

The gentle giant who breathed fire summoned his will and opened his mouth, but not a peep was made as flames shot out.

The witches joined hands and the ritual began. the air grew thick and tiny claws could be felt along their spines as the ground quaked beneath their feet. In the centre of the pyre a tear appeared, and glowing red eyes peered out, as a stunning man stepped through wearing a top hat, suit and a devilish grin to boot.

"Welcome home, Ring Master."

Do You Feel Lucky

Olaf was just finishing his errands when he spotted a figure. It was late, the gates were closed, and everybody was in the Ring Master's tent awaiting the feast to honour the special guest and her hounds.

The last thing Olaf wanted to do was chase down some punk kid, but he knew he'd lose more than his head if he walked away.

"Bloody kids."

Olaf was about to call it quits, when he saw a figure standing in the middle of the dodgem car tracks.

"Oi! You! The carnival is closed. You're trespassing."

"Do you feel lucky, Fire Breather?"

PICK POCKET

The thief shot through the crowd unseen; her movements swift like a bird flittering through the forest trees. She couldn't have been more than fourteen. On her third pass through the carnival, her pockets weighed down with jewels and wallets thick with cash, security finally caught onto the thief and attempted to corner her, unaware of the beasts that stalked their shadows waiting for their mistress's order to feast.

Lilith did not come to taunt the help, her business was with the Ring Master. But that didn't mean she wouldn't enjoy their human screams.

"Won't you play with me, Master?"

Survivor's Account

"It's okay, you're safe now. Tell us what you saw?" The Officer sat across from the witness.

"We were headed to the dodgems when the big guy saw us, so we ran and that's when we saw it. The trailer was glowing. Debi walked up to the window, I told her not too, but she looked inside and started screaming. The door open, and she appeared, smiling, and then the ground began to tremble, and there were dogs but we couldn't see them. Debi was still screaming, Sebastian was on his knees calling her his Queen! She's dead, isn't she?"

A Taste Of Toffee

The grounds should've been humming with life, laughter and excitement with a healthy dose of fear of the freaks. Instead there wasn't a soul insight. The carnival had been abandoned; the freaks confined to a cage.

Melted toffee glistened in the sun, ants rushed along in organised lines to and fro. Milky eyes stared unseeing as ants crawled out of orifices, and over the trapped remains of their own caught within the sticky sweetness.

Atop the fleshless skull, covered in toffee, was the Ring Master's hat with a note.

He shouldn't have tried to play the game.

I win, again.

JEM McCUSKER

Jem McCusker lives in Ipswich with her two sons and husband. Her first book Stone Guardians the Rise of Eden was released in 2018. She is releasing Crossfire, a Novella in September 2019. She longs to be a full-time author, won't wear yellow and loves rabbits.

www.jemmccusker.com

CHAINED

I hear a mouse scurry by, my nostrils flare at its scent. I want to stop but we keep moving through the sea of faces. Some stare and point, others gasp in shock.

I give them a piece of my mind until the lash of leather puts me in my place again.

"Shut it." Master commands.

Metal digs into my throat as I'm yanked back across the bars. I swipe out in defence, securing my Master. My nostrils flare at his scent, I'm poised, ready for the hunt. His blood drips from my claws.

I am lion, hear me roar.

DELIGHT

I am rectangular and exact. Small hands treasure me, secreting me in their pockets. I lie in wait. The distraction will come and parents will glance away, only for a moment.

Is it a chorus of screams filling the air as the scissor ride flings itself up, down and around?

The dodgem cars, spinning and sliding across the make shift floor?

I grow bored in my prison of darkness. The sickly summer heat surrounds me, I begin to melt, seeping out of my packaging and attaching myself to the lining.

Quick fingers unwrap me.

I am poison in a bite.

Two Hands

The crowd roared with applause, bursting from their seats. Lady Scarlett flew, a picture of elegance and grace.

William caught her mid-air and the crowd whooped in delight.

"She's some woman." Bobby, one of the four net holders said in awe.

"I wouldn't mind flying high with her." Jim replied with a suggestive wink before rubbing his crotch.

My eyes flared, burning red. Jim broke the cardinal rule. Two hands on the net, always.

Rage filled me. I lay in my death pose, my leg twisted at an impossible angle. My spirit tried and failed to avenge me.

Two hands.

A Penny For Your Thoughts

"Let Madame read your future." She leaned forward suggestively, her index finger tracing her cleavage.

I placed my coins on the table and offered my palm.

She traced the lines with sharp, pointed nails.

"I see a life filled with adventures and many beautiful women." She looked up beneath heavy painted lashes.

"You told my friend you saw death for her, she never made it home." I removed my hand, slipping it into my pocket, around the knife.

"Youthful nonsense, I'm sure." A soft click sounded below the table moments before the bullet struck me.

"I see death for you."

DEATH HYMN

The marching band kicked off the festivities with a lively jazz number. The steady, rhythmic beat of the drum called to alcohol induced primal urges. Men and women swayed and sung as they followed along.

They wound their way through Sideshow Alley, their music an anthem calling to show patrons near and far. Seasoned stall vendors called to them with offers of prizes and delight.

Their minds were in a trance, at one with the music.

As the ground disappeared beneath them and they fell from the mighty cliff top, they continued to sing.

"Oh, when the saints, go marching..."

KB Elijah

A Brisbane lawyer on weekdays and a writer on weekends, K.B. loves exploring 'what if?' questions. K.B.'s debut fantasy anthology featuring genies, demons and time-travellers, *The Empty Sky*, is available on paperback and kindle. Join K.B., her two cockatiels, and her love of books on her Instagram page at @k.b.elijah.

https://books2read.com/u/mgGZ1D

Sliver

Distorted fragments of visitors resonate through me; the same muffled voices and blurry glimmers I've been plagued with for years. Gaudy clothing, sticky fingers pressed against my prison, shrieks of delight and confusion.

I wait.

A couple passes by, loud voices raised in a heated argument. His fist shoots out, knuckles crunching into my silver cage. But I don't mind. Decades I have been trapped, locked in a mirror in a room of them. Hidden by the reflections of the carnival visitors, ignored beyond what they came to see.

Now a crack. Now, *freedom*.

Now revenge: bloody, hot and sweet.

THE CLEVER ONES

A crunch, a delighted smile. Blue eyes light up blissfully and the father nods his thanks.

Idiot. You paid for your son's doom. The child ignores them both, father and vendor alike, his small hands plunging back into the box of hot, buttery popcorn. More crunches, more smiles.

That's all there will ever be, for the rest of his little life. Instant addiction to a substance incompatible with man's physiology, a taste so divine that it trumps all urges to breathe, sleep or live.

The vendor had no regrets. The clever ones knew not to accept food from the fae.

SPECTRES

Shadows take on forms of their own, huge creeping beasts that lap at the feet of unwary travellers and loom over even the tallest of trees. Tent flaps crack in the wind that howls around deserted stalls, nudging stale popcorn and tugging at paper tickets stamped into the hard earth. There's rust on the rides, mould on the toys, and decades of decay.

A graveyard.

"Come on," I sigh, taking my wife's hand. I'm ignored. Her eyes light up in expectation, rewarded at the stroke of midnight when life returns to the desolate sideshows.

"Welcome to the Night Carnival, humans."

DUCKS AND SNACKS

The girl's stained tongue pokes from the side of her small mouth as she directs her focus to her prey. Her hand quavers, steadies, shakes again as her concentration ebbs and flows. Her whole world narrows to a single twist of plastic.

There.

She cheers as the hook catches on the bobbing duckling, a cheerful grin plastered on its otherwise vacant face.

She holds her breath as the vendor gifts her the prize. It oozes warmth against her skin.

Just her luck: yet *another* severed tongue.

She sighs and eyes another duckling. Maybe this time she'll finally win a brain.

SHINNING, SHIMMERING, SPLENDID

They soar through the air, hands clasped, eyes closed. It's a beautiful night: a canvas of stars and zephyrs and magic. Wind dances on their skin, wispy fingers tugging at their hair as the couple soar in the ecstasy of flight and the aching emptiness of the sky.

He opens his eyes, watches hers flicker behind her eyelids. Drinks in alabaster skin, auburn locks.

They could travel forever like this, up and away. Up into the stars and beyond.

But all things that go up must come down, whether it be bird or plane or lovers on a malfunctioning rollercoaster.

ZOE MARKS

Zoe, newby writer, dreaming of travelling and writing full time. She is the mother of one rambunctious little boy and two defiant cattle dogs. If she's not working, writing or running around after her family she's probably napping. Her other favourite hobbies are water skiing and scuba diving.

DANTE

Opening night of the Carnival was always a drunken party. This is what Dante loved most about being a carnie, all he wanted was to travel and party. Ravana, the head carnie, only had one rule, to let him know if you saw a cross on someone's collarbone. Sure it was a weird rule and there were plenty of strange rumours about the leader, but today was another opening night and Dante was ready. He was not ready for twilight the next day when he rolled to kiss awake his latest conquest only to find a cross on her collarbone.

CLOUD

As they neared the end of the line to the Ferris Wheel a curious cloud started to form over the top. Still they had waited this long, rain or not they were reaching the top. The three of them filed into their baskets eagerly waiting to see the view. The higher they went the more they could see all the beautiful lights of the Carnival below. At the pinnacle of the wheel the cloud engulfed them, blocking out all the sights from below. With a sharp jolt they found they were no longer in their basket but on solid ground.

THE BIG TOP

Ever since she had the vision all she could think about was the rundown Carnival. Walking through the gates at midnight probably wasn't her best idea but she couldn't sleep so here she was. Market stalls in various stages of disrepair lead towards the broken rides and in the centre of them all was the big top, glistening perfect as if new. She felt herself being drawn into the massive tent. As she reached the centre of the arena she heard a voice chanting "de magia est in vobis". Suddenly she was lifted into the air surrounded by kaleidoscopic flares.

MUM'S CARNIVAL

Every June the Carnival came to town.
Bringing with it rides, markets and shows. Most
kids in town couldn't wait to go and see
everything, the only thing Milo wanted to see
was his mother. She left him to be raised by his
grandparents when his was five, promising that
when he turned fifteen, he could go with her.
When the Carnival returned so did his mum,
the greatest acrobat anyone had ever seen.
This year was different as Milo, now 15, was
ready to leave with his mum. He walked up to
the main gate where she stood, grief-stricken.

THE ROYAL CARNIVAL

5000 years ago humans had fun. There was laughter, and enjoyment.. All of this changed in the year 2100 when Earth was destroyed. Now every centennial of the mass evacuation all human crafts converge on the site of what was once Earth. The 50th convergence as planned to be a Carnival to bring back what once was. An event where anything goes. As the ships pulled into the location a sea of lights and ships appeared. The royal ship flanked by its explorers started to slow as it approached the mass. Nobody has yet noticed the dark mass behind it.

SHAN L. SCOTT

Shan. L. Scott is an Australian Author. She is a lover of writing, singing & cats. She can often be found in her den at the computer, one cat at her feet & the other by her side, nutting out the next part of her tale. Shan's stories are relatable, heartfelt & are sure to tug at your emotions.

www.shanlscott.com

www.facebook.com/secondsightseries

FERRIS WHEEL

The huge wheel groans as it turns laboriously, steel on steel, dry bearings, devoid of grease and oil. Spinning slowly, it grinds to a halt. Two lovers, candy floss in hand, alight the carriage and embrace as the safety bar is lowered into place.

A groan and the wheel begins to spin, ever so slowly, higher and higher, until they are at the top.

A breeze, carriage swinging, metal joints squeaking, a gust of wind, candy floss drops. Girl leans forward and the safety bar gives way. The carriage tilts wildly, a brief shriek, a gasp.

A soft thud.

Silence.

CLOWNS

Side to side, the gaping maw rolls. Back and forth, its red rimmed orifice hangs ajar and lifeless eyes stare unseeing at passers-by.

"Step right up, try your luck" the freak beckons, bamboo cane in tattooed hand.

A cautious boy tugs at his mother's arm, pointing warily at the bear hanging behind the rows of jaws.

"Mamma, I want," he whispers, barely audible above the din.

He steps up to a face, picks up a ball and pokes it into a cold hard mouth. It jams. A little hand reaches in, hungry teeth clamp down. Screams echo into the night.

MERRY-GO-ROUND

Round and around, animals bobbing up and then down. Bright lights flash and music trills, joyful laughter rings in the air. My grip is tight, a black horse beneath me. I glance to my left and the centre mirrors glint, my reflection distorted, face leering. A look to the right and the crowd streams by, my head swimming. The thrum of music grows louder, lights flicker in unison. I see a dark space open up ahead. A tiny tear in space and time, made by this magical merry-go-round. I travel forward and slip inside. The portal closes, I am gone.

Jack In The Box

Smell of popcorn, animal dung, and sounds of squealing and laughter. I wander through the carnival, seeking my parents. Do they know I've gone? Will they find me again? I begin to cry. My tears fall in the dust as I pass between two large tents.

I spy the box, large, colourful, lever on the side and a sign that reads, "Wind me up."

I wind, the box pops open, a clown on a spring bounces back and forth. He swings forward wildly, grasps me suddenly in his cold embrace and pulls me into the box, I vanish into oblivion.

MIRRORS

Into the hall of mirrors I step, smiling with glee at my ridiculous appearance as glass bends, distorts and warps my figure and face. Further into the maze, feeling my way in the semi darkness, I catch a glimpse, someone behind me, watching, stalking. I hurry, frightened, around corners, through archways, all the while my disfigured face leering back at me from the mirrors. I halt, can go no further, a dead end lies before me. Turning, I gasp! The figure steps forward and pushes me roughly. I fall backward, into the glass and remain forever trapped within the mirror.

Monica Schultz

Monica Schultz is a History and Mathematics high school teacher, who loves to escape from her mundane life through novels. She can often be found writing young adult fantasy stories, with a cat curled on her lap, for anyone who also needs an escape from reality.

Instagram @miss.schultz

Twitter @MonicaSchultz_

Freak Show

I dig in my heels, desperately searching for an escape. The tent looms before us, gloved hands holding back the flaps to welcome the crowd.

I snatch my arm free. "Do we have to do this?"

My friends giggle at my pale face. "Come on, it'll be fun."

I swallow my fear and stare at the trampled grass to avoid the bright lights of the sign.

Freak Show.

My lungs grow heavy with every passing exhibit. I gasp for air. There he is. Waving to hecklers while he swims.

"Hi, Dad," I whisper.

Nobody knows mermaids develop legs on land.

HUNTED

Isabelle squints at the target. Muscles tense. She throws the final ball. *Ding, ding, ding!*

"That one," she grins, pointing at the glittering toy hidden behind a thin veil of smoke.

"Oh, no sweetheart, you can't have him," the carnie rasps. Her golden bangles clink as she reaches for an oversized teddy bear instead. The toy grins, flames slipping from between its razor-sharp teeth. A terrible actor.

"I said, that one," Isabelle growls, pulling the ancient dagger from her pocket. Orange eyes blink open in its scaly face. Zarr's pupils dilate in horror.

The hunters have found him once again.

SEA MONKEYS

Quinton's tongue pokes out of his mouth, his eyes screwed up as he squints at the prize. His hands tremble as he steadies the pole. *Dive!*

Quinton swoops down for his rubber duck. The yellow bugger swirls out of reach, bobbing on still water.

"Sea monkeys," Quinton curses, catching sight of their cheeky pink faces. They dart between ducks, laughing hysterically as children miss the perfect shot.

Splash. One jumps from the water, snatching a treat from the game master's fingers.

Quinton frowns, studying the trail of bubbles. Swift as a bird, he hooks a much sweeter prize; the cheater.

The Black Pen

The shed stinks of animals, the fresh layer of straw barely masking the reek of dung. Children squeal in delight as the calves lick between their fingers and the chickens flap out of reach.

"Wanna bite?" Rylan tosses an apple between his hands, taunting the lone piglet. Its tail twitches, but it doesn't turn.

He leans over the railing. *Crunch*. Sweet juice dribbles down Rylan's chin. He swipes it away, leaving a sticky trail on his sleeve. His arm dangles into the pen.

Red eyes flash. *Snatch*. The apple disappears behind razor teeth. Rylan screams. He should've read the sign.

When the Lights Go Out

Litter drifts on the wind, empty packets swirling around Alfryda's feet. Crows squabble over the food scraps squished into the trampled grass. A lone rat scurries. The remains of chaos a feast for hungry pests.

A single tear trickles down Alfryda's cheek as she rests in the faint silhouette of an enormous ride. Her wings droop, the sparkle fading from her eyes. They are so reckless with her homeland.

Yet, she cannot forget the joy. The nights of endless laughter. The days of squeals and cheers. Her heart swells with the memories of Sideshow Alley.

Maybe they'll care next year.

JAYNE VIDLER

Jayne is a mum of three and a lactation consultant who had a third life crisis and decided to follow a childhood dream of becoming an author. Jayne loves reading, writing and daydreaming up new wonderful book ideas. Her home is full of books and 3 young aspiring authors.

The Carnival Night Guard

The job was simple, keep the thrill-seeking teens, opportunistic thieves and sabotaging competition out. Tonight though, hinted at something menacing. A breeze blew through the carnival as the night guard made her rounds of side-show stalls and tents, scanning dark corners for lurking trouble.

As she rounded the corner of a building, gravel crunching stalled her advance. Flattening herself against the wall, she waited as footsteps approached. Hair stood up on the back of her neck and her heart drummed faster as the dark figure stepped into view, glowing red eyes flashed as the figure locked her in its sights.

Fated Tarot

The tarot cards are flipped, presenting Jill with the supposed answers to her questions. She gazes upon the cards, then up at the tarot reader. The reader, lips pressed together thinly, brow furrowed in concern, focuses on one card in particular. The Death card, a skeleton clad in black, riding a white horse.

As Jill focuses on the card, its sides began shimmering and a vision of her death unfolds as she stares in horror. Gasping, she stands abruptly sending her chair toppling to the ground.

"I can offer you an alternative?" a wicked smile plays on the reader's lips.

Show Bag Treats

The smell of the perfume she had gotten in the show bag as a girl, sat strong in her memory. She remembered sounds of the side-show heard from her bedroom window and watching the fireworks from her patio.

Those had been simpler times, a carefree child, relishing the show streets away from her home. Revelling in the memory, she held the perfume bottle, found at the bottom of an old chest.

Popping the cap, she inhaled deeply and felt a magical tingle spread through her body, transforming her aged frail figure back into the little girl she once was.

The Hustle

My body is bone achingly weary. A moment of weakness, the promise of eternal youth and now trapped, forever. The outside appears young, unchanged from my 20-year-old self, inside is another story. I sit staring at the mirror, examining, looking for the telltale signs of age. A wrinkle, a crease, a spot, nothing.

It hasn't changed since that day. I traded my soul for this decades ago. I thought it would buy my freedom. I was wrong. From one terrible situation smack bang into another.

She had promised me this carnival was the answer and it was, just not mine.

THE CARNIVAL OF SOULS

Gravel grinds under her boots as she walks the side-show, a breeze ruffling her coat tails. Her carnival, in all its glory, is most tantalizing at night, when all that is left are the souls trapped by her power. Each city, each stop, they add to the count.

They work the carnival, entrapping others with a trinket, a mystic reading or a promise. Eternal youth in exchange for a century of servitude, though none have yet to escape the enchantment. Her eyes flash red as movement catches her eye.

Another soul to add to her collection, her 'Carnival of Souls'.

J A HENDERSON

Jan-Andrew (J.A.) Henderson is the author of 24 teen, YA and adult. Published in the UK, USA, Germany, Australia and the Czech Republic, he has been shortlisted for thirteen literary awards and is the winner of the Doncaster Book Prize and Royal Mail Award.

He lives in Brisbane.

ALL DOGS GO TO HEAVEN

"I want you to give Plookie here a soul," Doris patted the Daschund at her feet. "All dogs should go to heaven."

"I only tell fortunes." Madam Zozo peered over her crystal ball.

"Google begs to differ." Doris dropped $5000 on the table. Zozo's eyes widened.

"I must use ze soul of someone who loves him. You ok viz zat?"

"Course. I adore the li'il tyke."

"Righto then." Zozo waved her arms theatrically. "Nagoobootowackamole. Give this pooch his owner's soul!"

The Daschund burped.

"All done. Take your dog and go."

"Oh, it's not mine," Doris shrugged. "Belongs to my ex-husband."

HARRY FRITSCH

Harry is a creative and professional writing graduate from QUT. He spends way too much of his time pacing around his flat in Ipswich, thinking up stories. However, the neighbours haven't complained yet, and so Harry has published video game articles and reviews for a variety of websites and is working on a fantasy novel in his spare time. That's when he's not pacing, of course.

Big Boy Rides

'Go!'

Scott was off.

He steered his dodgem into the swirling storm of cars.

He collided with a little girl and she seemed even smaller after the impact.

He charged another vehicle, they bounced, and Scott was now eye to eye with the man driving it.

Scott laughed and kept slamming into cars until they all looked like toys to him. His dodgem now blocked the entire circuit.

Everything fell under his shadow. His mother had fussed over him not being tall enough for a "Big Boy" ride. He smiled down at her.

I wonder if she might listen now.

Inside Out Lunch

'Hey, mister. What's in that showbag, the brown paper one?'

'Why boy, that's no showbag, that's my lunch! Two Dagwood Dogs smothered in tomato sauce.'

'Why two, mister? I don't see anyone else with you.'

'I see two of us, though. What do you say, boy? One for me, one for you?'

'I-I'm not sure. I've already eaten today.'

'Just a bite, I promise they're tasty. Here. Try one.'

'O-Okay, thanks, mister. Boy, these sure are tasty! Ahem. Sorry to keep you waiting. What can I get for you, boy?'

'Hey, mister. What's in that showbag, the brown paper one?'

INFLAMED PRICES

It was night-time, and of all the shops on Sideshow Alley, this was the only one with no lights on. Instead, there lay a box of candles outside its locked door. So, I took one and used my lighter to ignite the wick.

Now everything else in the show went dark and the shop burst into neon colour. The door swung open and a round man sauntered out.

'You took the candle,' he said, grinning. 'You know what that means?'

'Oh, I'm afraid I don't.'

He thrust out his hand, nearly making me drop the candle. 'That'll be $35, thanks.'

The Violinist

Have you heard the violinist? She only plays in the rain.

When the water comes down and the "Closed" signs come out, she's in the middle of the alley, playing her songs. The speakers cease and the crowd gathers under shelter, listening.

She always smiles at the children, even when her music is sad. And, her yellow dress shines in the gloom, never taking any of the rain which falls around her.

But, when the rain stops, so does the violinist. The speakers start up and the crowd returns to the attractions.

And the sun smiles instead, warm as music.

ABOVE AND BEYOND

The Ferris wheel had broken down while we were right at the top. We should've been able to look over the carnival from our little cabin, but a heavy fog had rolled in and masked the lights and colours from below. The nervous chatter between my friends had ended and we all just stared out into the mist, silent.

Slowly, the fog began to thin. I smiled as I looked for the people on the ground. But there were no people. Only stars.

It was never fog. These were clouds. And we were now above them, floating into the night.

JASMINE JARVIS

Teller of tales, scribbler of scribbles. I have been writing since 2011, only recently deciding to try my hand at writing fiction. I reside in Brisbane, Queensland, with my family (aka my muses).

Authentic Oddities

Here in my tent in sideshow alley, I am very careful as I set out the assortment of glass jars that are filled with oddities floating in sepia coloured preserving fluid. Bulbous eyes, fins, tails, fangs and claws, fur and scales. Half and half creatures of my own creation. The light bulb overhead sways, throwing shadows just the way I need it to - to hide the stitching and wires holding these creatures together, fooling the crowds into believing that these things are indeed real and out there waiting to get them.

I am very proud of my "authentic" oddities.

Opening Night Nerves

Opening night and I am nervous. Despite doing this performance every night since I was a little girl, I still feel butterflies in my tummy before I have to step out onto that small, rickety wooden stage.

The reactions of the audience no longer bother me for back in my caravan waits my love, and to him I am perfection. The Emcee pokes his head in to tell me it is time, and I stand up to straighten out my dress.

I give my beard one final brush out before stepping out onto the stage to sate the audience's curiosity.

See The Fire

The outdoor stage in sideshow alley was lit up by strands of fairy lights, casting an ethereal feel to the final show on the last night of the circus. Music started and suddenly the night sky was ablaze as Little Dragon leapt onto the stage; the flames twirling about her tiny frame. The young girl in the crowd was mesmerised – in a time where she was expected to grow up and become wife and homemaker, Little Dragon with her flames, lit up her mind, showing her another life, drawing the young girl to see the fire within her own heart.

Sideshow Alley

The air is rich with the scent of buttered popcorn, fairy floss and of the jungle creatures that pace back and forth in their cages waiting for their turn in the ring. To avoid the noise, I dart down into sideshow alley – lit up with fairy lights strung up between the rows of tents. Behind each tent flap hides an otherworldly curiosity to behold. A hand pops out from one of the entryways and it beckons for me and I approach its tent.

As I enter, I fail to see the sign that reads "BEWARE of the always hungry WEREWOLF!"

The Tattooed Man

When I was a little boy, my Ma had saved up enough pennies to take me to the circus.

I will never forget it was in sideshow alley where I saw a man who was covered head to toe in tattoos that *moved*. I had never seen anything like him before. A snake slithered up his right arm, the island girl on his stomach waved and blew me a kiss.

A ship sailed in the turbulent sea across his shoulders. Blue birds flittered on his neck, and a devil on his chest with flames in its eyes, winked at me.

SOFIA AVES

Sofia Aves loves to write and see new talent emerge around Brisbane. She leads the team at Little Quail Press and writes romance in her spare time.

www.LittleQuailPress.com

Sofia's Sweet Sirens:

https://facebook.com/groups/36588922 4364512/?ref=share

FACADES AND FLOWERS

Dim light filtered with dirt and dust shone on the lone caravan. Bright with its cheery, red spoked wheels, walls adorned with blue and yellow flowers. Swirls decorated its curved door in a welcoming manner.

Set apart from the rest of the carnie's cluster of white vans, this caravan was distinctly Rom.

But if you looked carefully, turning in the light just so, there was a darkness, a shadow that hid in the edges of the bright paint, crept through the cracks in the boards.

Sometimes, the flowers moved.

The darkness wasn't Rom in the least.

Just a pretty fascade.

PRACTICE ROUNDS

"They're screaming. Again."

Lila clung to the post, hiding beneath the half-erected canvas of the tent.

"Don't you worry, lass. Just practicing for the magic show."

Lila frowned. She'd never heard screams like that during the performance. She stared into the gnarled face of the old carnie. Sadness swirled in his eyes as he stared into hers, colours running together.

He tousled her dirty blonde curls, resting his hand on her head for a moment. He grabbed the canvas, stealing her safety, whistling. She stared into the van, knowing her eyes swirled just like his.

Magic didn't need practice here.

Aim True

"Oh, that was a wonderful shot, dear."

Her shrivelled hands tugged the dart free, palming the number beneath. Counting backwards with the lad, she doled out his remaining darts, slipping an extra one in with a quick glance over her shoulder.

"Aim true," she whispered as he threw. One more withered balloon. "Last one. Make it good." She whispered the words again, his balloon bursting with a show of confetti and glitter.

She avoided the carnie's gimp eye, hiding trembling hands, presenting the ecstatic lad with a large, plush dinosaur. A happy child with a huge toy was always worthwhile.

NICOLE HARVEY

Nicole Harvey is a writer who loves all things language and reading. When she's not writing she dips her toe into unusual things like reading about death, enjoying running, and medieval re-enactment.

https://www.facebook.com/nicole.harveyauthor

www.instagram.com/nicoleharvey136

Joey's First Ride

"Slow down Joey." But Joey couldn't resist racing ahead.

"I think I'm tall enough for the Spooky Coaster." He gasped at the bright lights and the scary music.

"Are you okay, baby?" He hadn't realised he'd stopped.

"I'm not a baby!" Joey pulled his mum to the sign. "Look, I reach now."

Joey bought a ticket and found himself first in line, bouncing on the spot. He ignored the music as the ride went up and his mum got smaller. He let go with one hand to show her he was ok. BANG!

Joey kept waving as she grew closer.

Haunted House

Dressed in full zombie costumes we slip into the haunted house. Half the fun is scaring the paying customers. The fools think they can handle it... until they realise the characters are real.

I've saved the biggest shock of all for Dave. The knife I slipped into my pants will make sure of that. I find the perfect spot. He only sees it at the last second. Eyes wide but it's too late. Propped against the wall, he blends right in. I slip behind a curtain and listen.

"Best haunted house ever!"

"I know right, the blood looks so real."

A Child's Eyes

I see red, blue, lellow. Purple and green. In the lights. In the toys. Up on the shelf, he's my favourite by far. With a fat long tail and stripes so thick, he stands proud and tall. What's his colour? Mummy knows. I turn to tug her shirt. It's not there, it was blue. I whirl between the legs, my heart thuds. A hand grabs me, I see her face. I smile again.

As we leave the stand, she tells me. My new favourite is orange. He's tucked under my arm, I'm tucked under mummy's.

The safest place I know.

SILVIE DE WILDE

Silvie de Wilde is an emerging writer who enjoys exploring the gothic and magical realism. She's ventured into other mediums previously but most notably poetry which also influences her writing style. You can often find Silvie in the bottom of her garden with dogs and chooks, contemplating the next story idea.

www.facebook.com/silviedewildeauthor
www.instagram.com/silvie_de_wilde

FUNNY FACE

Gisella had been stood up on her 137th blind-date, the day she fell in love.

"Watch out, Funny Face," spat a drunk stumbling into Gisella.

His companion whooped pointing to poster, "Yeah, the circus is in town." She pushed past them into the bar.

"What'll it be?" the barman asked.

"Whisky and milk."

"Make it two," said another. Rust tufted hair, a bulbous nose blotchy from drink and tears that'd etched his makeup.

He looked as she did.

"Have to run away with me sweet cheeks. Never met anyone else who takes melancholy's cure the way I do," he slurred.

Magnus Moreau's Fine Statue Show

Stage lights backlit the audience, that even the smallest hair could be seen standing on end. John had forgotten his earlier complaint on staying out that night, "...but love, tomorrow's Magnus Moreau's Fine Statue Show."

This was electric.

"Now, ladies and gentlemen, I must ask you to place on your blindfolds. At no point are you to remove them as you experience the most beautiful, otherworldly sound of Serena."

John's blindfold slips and he can't resist a look before turning to stone.

The following morning a woman runs a nail across his surface declaring, "Darling, he's *perfect* for the garden."

DANCING BEAR

She dances clumsily to a medieval tune,
beady eyes taking in the full house. When she
sees Nikolay, she stumbles. Owner pulls on
her muzzle with a warning face.

She looks foolish but Nikolay applauds,
so she continues performing just for him. When
a woman sits beside him, she recognises
Vasilka her betrayer, keeper of this curse.

The clock begins striking midnight. With
the roaring crowd, Owner's not kept a close
eye on the time. She stands to her full height,
bellowing. In a moment, she'll return to her
human form but with a mind of the wild,
revenging bear.

The Fortune-Teller

"This is the first we are to meet, my uncle and I. Then we'll be travelling together," the girl explains.

The fortune-teller with ring laden fingers grasps the child's hand tighter when the vision of broken tracks comes. She observes carriages skittled across a white forest. She observes the absence of breath on a below freezing night.

Sitting upright, the fortune-teller discards the hand. "No charge this evening," she mutters, ushering the girl out.

Later as the circus train boards, the fortune-teller finding her seat fails to notice the girl holding her uncle, the ringmaster's hand.

A snowflake falls softly.

The Judas Kiss

Tangled in the sheets, they fall apart.

"Contortionists have *all* the moves," the tattooed man smirks, lighting a cigarette.

Ana begins tracing his ink work but when she comes to a particular tattoo, he grabs her hand.

"The Judas Kiss," he explains. "Someone betrayed me once. It's to remind me I'll never do the same."

She leans over and takes a drag of his cigarette.

"You don't smoke!" he says.

"Karina *doesn't* smoke. All your canoodling in dark corners of the big top, and still you can't tell the difference between us twins," Ana muses blowing smoke in his face.

CONTRIBUTORS

DANIELLE DOOLITTLE

Danielle Doolittle lives in Toledo, Ohio, with her husband, four children and two very active dogs. When she's not acting as a full-time in-house supervisor, (sounds so much more official than stay-at-home-mom), she can be found with a graphics pen in hand, bringing other author's stories to life visually. When she's not designing covers, Danielle also writes her own books.

She loves coffee, dark chocolate and Twitter. Not necessarily in that order (okay, pretty much in that order).

ROZIE MARSHALL

Rozie Marshall is a caffeine-fuelled, chip junkie author with entirely too much time on her hands. She has been driven crazy by one husband, two children, and four fur babies. She loves poetry, long walks on the beach, and candlelit dinners; as long as the meds are still in her system. If the meds have worn all, for the love of sex and sin, RUN...

https://www.facebook.com/RozieMashall/

https://www.facebook.com/groups/RozieMarshallBooks/

https://www.amazon.com/Rozie-Marshall/e/B07Q3SCZV4?ref=sr_ntt_srch_lnk_1&qid=1560627142&sr=8-1

ACKNOWLEDGEMENTS

So many people went into creating this book. Only a few years ago, I resumed the writing journey I'd started as a child. My dream, even back when I was eleven, was to become a published author. I loved reading and had lots of stories to share.

That creative flow never stopped and with support from local groups, I was included in a few anthologies and connected with people who have helped further my dream. Several book launches and multiple Facebook groups later, I realised there were a lot of Ipswich unpublished and emerging authors who doubted their creativity. I wanted to help, to give local writers - you! – confidence, and Sideshow Alley was born. I had plenty of my own doubts going in, prepared for the idea to bellyflop. The response and enthusiasm I received from local authors was astounding! So, we got here, thanks to those writers, many of whom never thought they would never see their work published. Congratulations on getting your work out there and for taking that leap of faith. Writers, *authors* – this is YOUR book!

Many thanks for support and enthusiasm goes to the writers of the Springfield Writers Group and Ipswich Writers & Illustrators Group. Without you, this book wouldn't exist at all.

To my Author Harem girls – Bo, Jodie, Serena, Winter, Jill, Maya, Leanne, Dani, Natasja, Erica & MJ – thank you for boosting me back into the saddle when I fell, mud splattered and grass stained, but you pulled me back up and gave me a shove int eh right direction.

Craig – thank you for tech support and helping me install a dvd player for my own sanity. It was tougher going than I thought!

To Danielle, thank you for answering all my questions and just being awesome. Rozie, thank you for coming on board last minute and saving my behind!

To my amazing husband, thank you, for blinking bleary eyes and agreeing vaguely when

I yelled out at five am one frigid morning about circuses and sideshows...and for supporting me the whole way. To my fabulous kids and lounge shark/muse Kala – thank you for redecorating my keyboard with an assortment of foods and liquids. Sticky keys are much more fun this way.

And last, but never, EVER, least: unlimited thanks to my Four Quills ladies. Thank you for supplying me with coffee, conversation and incredible support when I broke a few times. For celebrating wins with me big and small and making me feel just a little more "normal" every day. Love you guys xxx